MARTHA SPEAKS™

Funny Bone
Jokes and Riddles

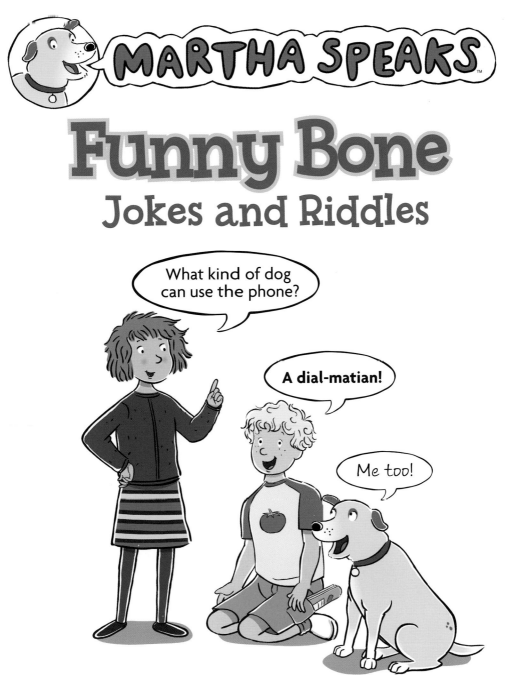

What kind of dog can use the phone?

A dial-matian!

Me too!

Written by Karen Barss
Based on the characters created by Susan Meddaugh

HOUGHTON MIFFLIN HARCOURT
Boston • New York • 2013

Knock, knock.

Woo.

AGES	GRADES	GUIDED READING LEVEL	READING RECOVERY LEVEL	LEXILE® LEVEL
5–7	2	J	17	410L

For information about permission to reproduce selections from this book, write to Permissions, Houghton Mifflin Harcourt Publishing Company, 215 Park Avenue South, New York, New York 10003.
Library of Congress Cataloging-in-Publication Data is on file.

ISBN: 978-0-547-86579-9 pb
ISBN: 978-0-547-86577-5 hc

Design by Lauren Zwicker.

www.hmhbooks.com
www.marthathetalkingdog.com

Manufactured in China
SCP 10 9 8 7 6 5 4 3 2 1
4500384902

How does Martha stop the DVD player?

She presses the "paws" button!

Hey! I was watching that.

What do dogs have that no other animal has?

Puppies!

What goes "woof, woof, tick, tick"?

A watchdog.

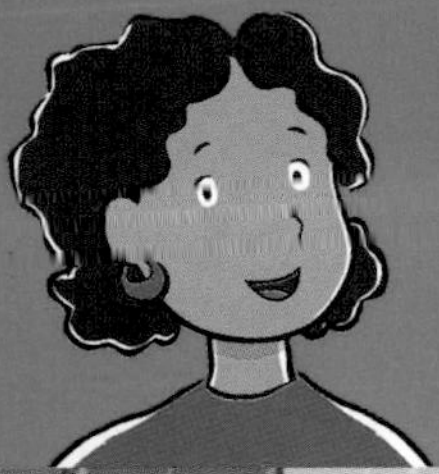

Why do you have to be careful when it rains cats and dogs?

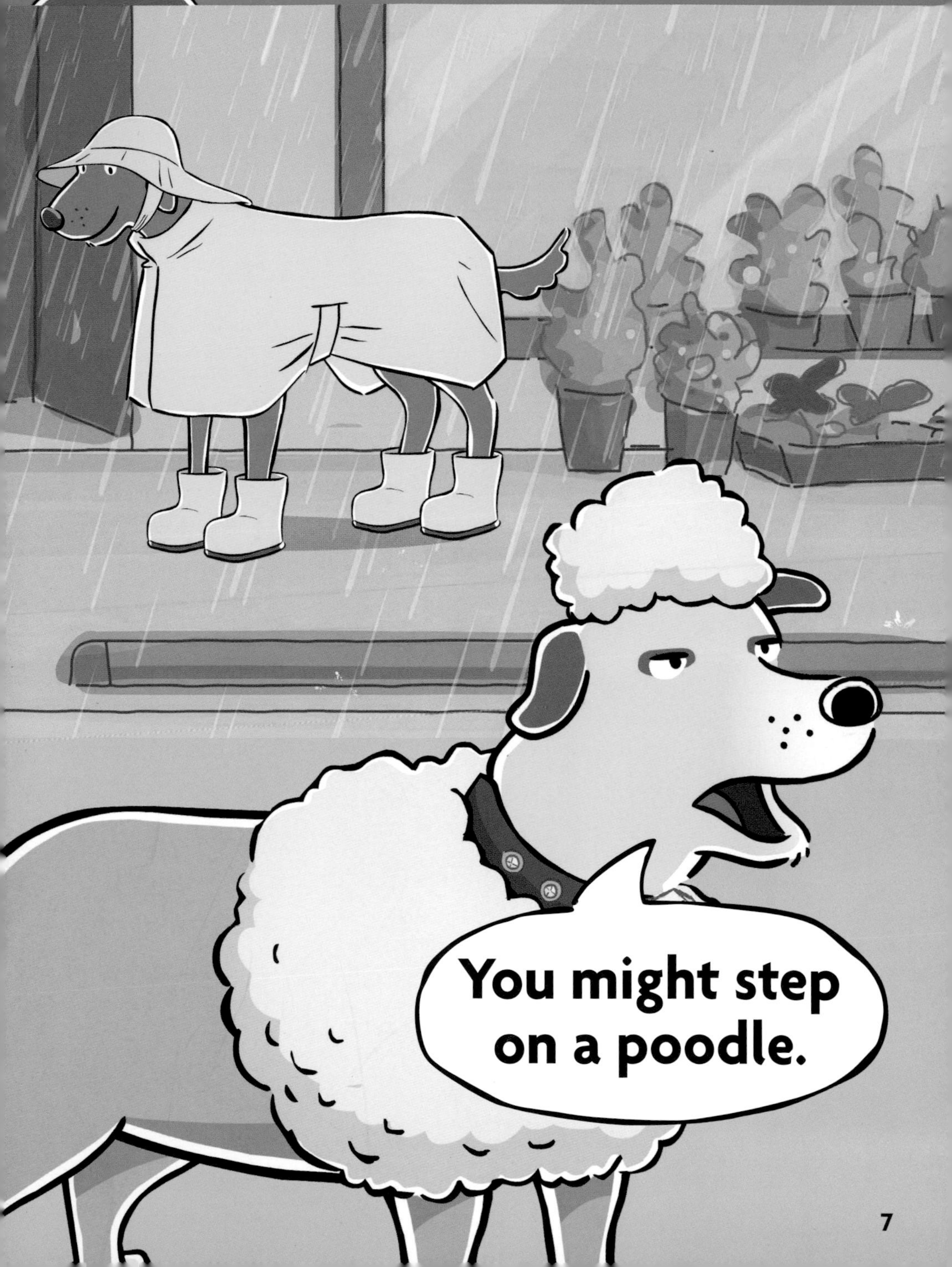

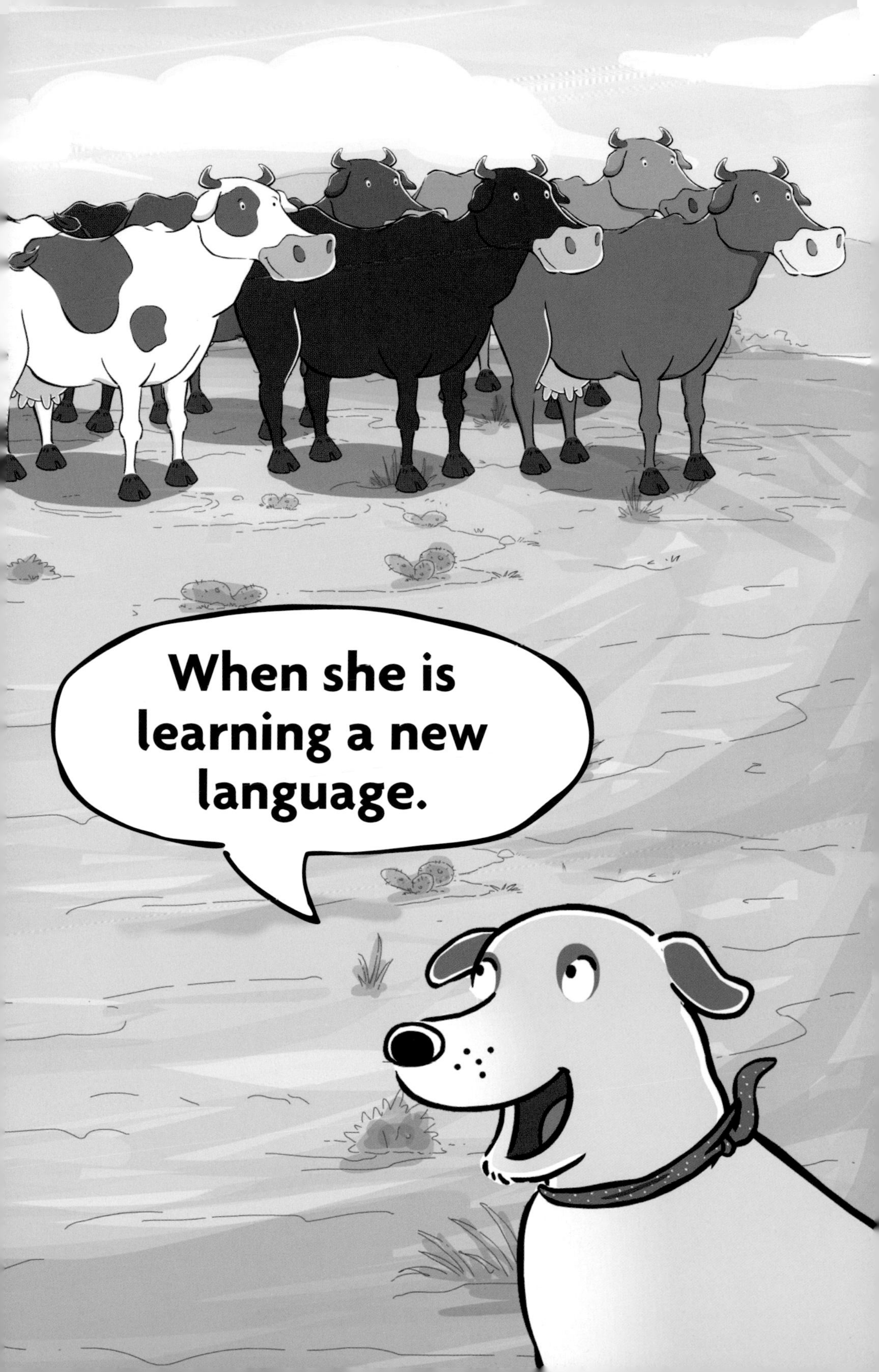
When she is learning a new language.

What kind of dog loves
to take a bath?

A shampoodle!

What do you get if you cross a hot dog, a dog, and Dracula?

Hotdogula!

Why are Dalmatians bad at hide-and-seek?

They are always spotted!

Why is it called a "litter" of puppies?

Because they mess up the whole house!

What do ducks like to watch on TV?

The feather forecast.

What kind of dog should you invite to a tea party?

A teacup poodle!